Shakespeare Tales

Twelfth Night

First published 2016 by

Bloomsbury Education, an imprint of Bloomsbury Publishing Plc
50 Bedford Square, London, WC1B 3DP

www.bloomsbury.com

Bloomsbury is a registered trademark of Bloomsbury Publishing Plc
Text copyright © Terry Deary 2016
Illustrations © Tambe 2016

A CIP catalogue for this book is available from the British Library

ISBN: 978-1-4729-1783-6 (paperback)

Printed and Bound by CPI Group (UK) Ltd, Croydon CR0 4YY

1 3 5 7 9 10 8 6 4 2

MIX
Paper from
responsible sources
FSC® C020471
FSC
www.fsc.org

TERRY DEARY

Shakespeare Tales

Twelfth Night

Illustrated by
Tambe

BLOOMSBURY EDUCATION
AN IMPRINT OF BLOOMSBURY
LONDON OXFORD NEW YORK NEW DELHI SYDNEY

Contents

Prologue

Richmond Palace, 6th January 1601
The girl's tale

An iron man guarded the door to the palace. He scared me. John the wine-server laughed at me. 'It's only a suit of armour, Maid Jane. There's nothing inside. He can't hurt you.'

The armour hand held a heavy iron ball on a wooden stick. 'It's called a mace,' John told me. 'Knights used them to smash the heads of their enemies.' I shivered and ran past the hollow, metal man. John ran after me, giggling. 'The Queen's father used to wear that armour. He was called Henry

the Eighth and they say his ghost still haunts it.'

I raced down the cobwebbed corridors – no one cleaned those parts of the palace that only the servants could see. I was late already. She's be cross. There was a crowd arriving. I pushed through the stiff dresses of the grand ladies and the swords of the gentlemen that hung by their belts. They were all heading into the great hall to see the play. They were chattering and laughing, so pleased to be invited to the palace.

There was a sudden hush. The lords and ladies froze in the cold air and began to lower their heads. My Lord the Earl of Essex was entering with his bodyguards. He was the Queen's favourite and no one dared to look him in his proud eye. He swept through to the door.

An old steward with a grey beard stepped across the doorway. 'Sorry, My

Lord, but nobody may enter the same room as Queen Elizabeth wearing their sword.'

'I'm not nobody,' Lord Essex said and barged past with his gang of bullies. The waiting crowd gasped and gossiped as they shuffled into the hall to take their seats. 'He wants to be king,' John hissed in my ear before he hurried off to serve wine to the guests.

The Queen was old now – the warrior who once led England against Spanish enemies was fading like a dying candle. And her palace was crumbling.

Still she painted her face and dressed in her jewels as if she were a young princess. But the few teeth she had left were black and her skin was like crumpled paper. She walked hunched over a stick and gasped for breath. The palace was falling into ruin and no one cared; no one was scared of her any longer.

The gossips said Lord Essex wanted to sit on the throne of England – even if it meant dragging old Queen Elizabeth off it by force. As we sat to watch Master Shakespeare's new play, 'Twelfth Night', there was fear in the hall like a fog making the air thick.

Queen Elizabeth entered. I took a seat in the shadows. The actors leapt into the torchlight and the story began...

Act 1

Sea and storm
The play

A beach in Illyria

The wind is from the west, whipping the waves like froth on a boiling pot. The sailing ship creaks then cracks and the foaming water washes the poor passengers into the cold sea. Lashing grey waves crash against the stony beach and blow a girl ashore, more dead than alive. She is Viola.

'What country is this?' she asks the

Captain who's just rescued her from the cruel waves.

'This is Illyria, lady,' he tells her.

'Have you seen my twin bother, Sebastian? He was on the ship with me. I was saved. Maybe he will be too.' she moans.

'Maybe he will,' the Captain says but the sailors shake their heads.

'Who is the ruler of Illyria?' the weary girl asks.

'Duke Orsino,' the Captain says. 'A sad man.'

'Sad? He rules this country. Why would he be sad?'

The Captain gives a great sigh. 'He's sad because he loves the Lady Olivia. But Olivia's father and brother have both died. She's miserable and can't be bothered with men.'

'Is everyone here miserable?' Viola cries. 'If I went as a servant to Lady Olivia I may be able to cheer her sad life.'

The Captain shrugs, 'She won't see any strangers.'

'Then I'll serve the Duke Orsino,' the girl says. 'I'll pretend to be a boy. Help me disguise myself.'

And so Viola dresses as a boy and

goes to work for Orsino. She calls herself Caesario and becomes his favourite servant. He trusts her so much he sends her off on a special job. She has to go to the sad Olivia and persuade her to marry Orsino. A job that is nearly impossible. Olivia won't even listen to Orsino's messengers.

Still Viola will try because she is secretly very fond of her new master. She must get Olivia to marry Orsino... even though Viola would rather marry him herself!

Olivia's palace is home to some strange people. First there is her idle, boastful uncle, Sir Toby Belch. What a waster.

Then there is his straw-haired friend with half a wit, Sir Andrew Aguecheek. Such a fool.

The head servant is Malvolio, such a pompous, puffed up man who never saw a joke. Oh so pitiful.

Olivia's servant is Maria, a playful, saucy maid. She makes trouble.

The girl's tale

I sat on a cushion on the floor beside the door. I loved to watch Maria on the stage. When I grew older I wanted to be like her. Full of fun and scared of no one. But as a maid to Elizabeth I lived in fear – fear of her frightening temper and fear that her worst terrors were true – the Queen's dread that someone would kill her.

Lord Essex whispered something in her
ear. I saw her smile then hide her rotting
teeth behind a fan. While the guests all
watched the play I watched Lord Essex.
He gave a secret look to his four guards.
They gripped the handles on their daggers.
Waiting for some sign. Could there be a
plot? Or maybe I was being foolish. I kept
watching Mr Shakespeare's wonderful
play. I jumped as John the wine-server sat
beside me.

'What's happening?' he asked.

'Viola's come to ask Olivia to marry her master, Orsino. Now hush. Let's see what happens.'

Olivia says she will not see the messenger from Orsino. But Viola, dressed as Caesario, says she will build a cabin at the palace gate and stay forever if she has to. Olivia starts to love the messenger Caesario. She loves him more than she can ever love Orsino. She wants to see the girl-boy again. 'Go back to your lord. I can't love him. Tell him not to send any more messengers – unless you feel like coming back to tell me how he took the news?'

Oh what confusion, what a tangle, what a jumble. Olivia loves the boy Caesario who's not a boy but a girl, Viola. Viola loves Orsino but Orsino loves Olivia.

More muddled than a muddy puddle... but the strange tale will get still muddier, you'll see...

Plots and play

The girl's tale

As the audience laughed at the tale on stage I saw five men with faces like frozen mud – Lord Essex and his four guards. Their eyes were on the stage but their thoughts were somewhere else.

'I don't like them,' I whispered to John. I expected him to mock me but he nodded slowly.

'They are plotting something,' he agreed. 'But what can four men do?'

'Four men with swords and daggers

against people in armour of velvet and silk.' I reminded him.

'We'll think of something,' he said.

'Will we?' I asked.

'Oh, yes,' he said. 'We know they are up to something but they don't know we know. We can surprise them.'

I scratched my head. 'It sounds more mixed up than Master Shakespeare's play.'

And that play was getting more twisted than a hangman's rope...

The play

Back in Illyria, Sebastian — Viola's twin brother — has come safely ashore from the shipwreck. He is sure Viola must have died. Here he is, stranded in a strange land. He sets off to see if Duke Orsino can help him. He's the same Orsino that has given Viola a job taking messages to Olivia.

In Olivia's palace Viola is in more danger than she knows. Olivia is so fond of her she treats Viola like a favourite friend. And that makes her drunken uncle, Sir Toby, quite upset. So he and the serving girl Maria come up with a plot to drive

Viola out. They will challenge Viola to a sword-fight with Sir Andrew. That'll get rid of her.

But there is another plot brewing and stewing in Maria's wicked mind. The chief servant, Malvolio, is complaining about Sir Toby getting drunk with his limp friend Sir Andrew Aguecheek. Maria has a plan to get revenge on the puffed-up, pompous, petty Malvolio.

So many plots. Maria is sure that Malvolio adores their mistress, Olivia. The great lady would never marry a sour, mean, miserable man like him. But what if he *thought* she loved him too?

What if Maria wrote a letter and pretended it was from Olivia?

What if the letter said Olivia would love Malvolio... if only he would smile and wear bright clothes? What if the letter said that if Malvolio would wear yellow stockings with crossed garters then Olivia would love him for all time?

The truth is Olivia hates yellow and crossed garters. She is so sad since her brother died that she hates to see people smile. A smile on his vinegar face will make him look an ass, a beef-wit and a bird-brain.

And what if they dropped the letter in the path of Malvolio and let him read it? Maria goes off to write the lying letter.

It's another twist in this tale. As you know, Olivia loves the boy Caesario who's

not a boy but a girl, Viola. Viola loves Orsino but Orsino loves Olivia. Now, to make the comedy complete, the gloomy servant Malvolio loves Lady Olivia too.

Next day the jokers hide in the garden of Olivia. They see Malvolio coming, they

drop Maria's letter on the path and then they hide and wait to see the fun. As it happens Malvolio is thinking about Lady Olivia.

He mutters to himself, 'Maria once told me Olivia was fond of me. I've almost heard Olivia say that herself. She said if she were to love anybody, it would be someone who looked like me.'

The plotters try to smother their giggles. 'Be quiet,' Sir Toby Belch tells Sir Andrew.

'I'd be Count Malvolio,' the chief servant says with a dreamy sigh.

And then he finds the letter. He's sure his lady loves him. **'I thank my stars I am happy,'** he cries. 'I will smile. I will do everything the letter asks me to.'

He dashes off to find some yellow stockings and fix a grin on his sour face. Poor man. The joke is very cruel. The plotters loved their joke. Now it's time to drive Viola out, Plot number two.

The girl's tale

That's when the actors took a break and John jumped to his feet to gather up his wine jar and start to serve the great guests in the hall.

The Earl of Essex sat beside the Queen and kissed her hand and looked at her as a hungry wolf looks at a rabbit pie. Like Sir Andrew in the play he didn't see a woman or a queen – he saw the pots of gold that would make him rich if he had her in his power.

The four frightening guards rose from their seats and wandered through the door. They spoke in low voices. 'The Queen has no soldiers here tonight to guard her?' one asked.

'Not one,' another said.

'That's perfect, then,' a third one said. 'Tonight's the night we strike.'

Garters and grins
The play

Viola returns to Lady Olivia to beg her to marry Lord Orsino. But Olivia doesn't want to listen. She thinks Viola, dressed as Caesario, is much too handsome. She asks Viola to return... any time.

That makes Sir Andrew Aguecheek pout and fret, sniffle and whine. 'Olivia treated the Duke's messenger better than she's ever treated me. I am wasting my time.'

'Of course she did,' Sir Toby Belch

laughs. 'She saw you there and wanted to make you jealous. It's you she really loves, Sir Andrew.'

'Does she?'

'Of course. And she will love you more if you tell the young man you want to fight with him. Hurt him in eleven places.'

Pale Sir Andrew turned whiter than a ghost. 'Will you ask the young man to fight me?'

'Write it down and I will take the message to him. Make it look strong and angry like a soldier. That will terrify him.'

And so Sir Andrew goes to write his message. And Maria has some news. Sour-faced Malvolio is dressed in yellow stockings and crossed garters with a twisted smile on his face. When he tells Lady Olivia how he loves her it will be so funny. Sir Toby cannot miss the joke.

The girl's tale

Queen Elizabeth laughed till she coughed. She caught my eye and made a sign to show she needed a drink. I slipped through the door to find John.

'Water and wine for Her Grace,' I said.

He nodded and poured quickly into a silver goblet. 'The play has stopped till she feels better,' I said as I took the cup.

'Let's hope the play goes on till the end,' John said.

'Because you think it's a great play?'

He looked cross. 'No because I still don't have a plan to save the Queen. Give her the wine and make sure she is well enough to sit there another hour. I may think of something.'

I hurried back into the hall. The Queen croaked, 'The smoke from the torches made me cough.'

Lord Essex seemed as worried as a rat

in a dog-fighting pit. 'Your Grace, you need to rest. Rest from the worries of wearing the crown.'

My mistress sipped her wine and turned her cold, dark eyes on the young lord. 'I am too young to retire,' she spat.

He bowed his head, silent... then looked across at his four guards.

'On with the play!' the Queen cried and all the great folk in the hall clapped for her.

The play

When Malvolio appears in yellow stockings, Olivia is shaken with terror. She is sure her chief servant is ill with a brain fever. **'Sweet lady, ho, ho,'** he cries with a crocodile grin on his face.

'Why are you smiling? You know how sad I am,' she asks.

'I can be sad if you want me to be,' he says. 'These crossed garters are hurting me so I can easily be sad when I think of them.'

'What is wrong with you? **Is there some**

darkness in your mind?' she asks.

'My legs may be yellow, but my mind is not dark,' he replies happily.

Just then Viola returns and Olivia dashes to see her. 'Take care of Malvolio,' she orders her uncle, Sir Toby.

And Toby Belch 'takes care' of Malvolio by locking him in a dark, dank dungeon like a madman.

Then Maria and Sir Toby turn to their other prank. They set up the fight between Sir Andrew Aguecheek and Viola. They find Viola in the garden. Sir Toby tells her she has upset Sir Andrew.

'There must be some mistake,' Viola says. 'I'm sure nobody would want to fight with me. I can't remember anything I've ever done to annoy anyone.'

'You're wrong,' Sir Toby says.

'Who is this man, Sir Andrew?' Viola asks and trembles.

'He is a knight and a real monster when he's fighting. He's a devil,' Sir Toby lies.

Then Sir Toby hurries off to find Sir Andrew and tells him just the same. 'That boy Caesario agreed to fight you. He's a wild warrior. He never misses with his sword.'

Sir Andrew sobs, 'I wish I'd never told him I want to fight.'

'Too late now,' Sir Toby says. 'He's waiting over there. Now draw your sword and fight.'

And so the fight begins. Two fighters, each too scared to strike a blow. They close their eyes and circle round and wave their swords. Whenever the swords touch they squeak and squeal and yelp and whine.

The fight is stopped when a ship's captain steps in to rescue Viola. Why?

Because he is the man who saved her twin brother Sebastian. He sees Viola dressed as a young man so he is sure Viola is Sebastian.

Now Viola is filled with joy. She knows her brother lived when the ship sank. She needs to find him. But where?

Wedding and wine

The girl's tale

John whispered in my ear. 'At the end of the play the Earl of Essex will lead the Queen away and tell the lords that she has given up the throne. He will tell everyone she is retiring. He will say wants him to rule England for her,' John said.

'He can't,' I said. 'He can't lead the Queen away *and* tell the lords he is taking over. Not at the same time.'

John rolled his eyes. 'He will get his bodyguards to take the Queen away.'

I took a deep breath. 'So... if we get rid of the bodyguards we spoil his plot,' I said.

He looked at me as if I had lost my mind in a fog on the Thames. 'A boy and a girl against four armed men? How do we do that?' he sneered.

'Easy. The play shows us how,' I said with a small smile. 'Get me a set of your best clothes. I need to dress as a boy, just like Viola.'

43

The play

Viola's brother arrives at the palace of Olivia. Of course Sir Toby Belch is sure this is Viola come back. The young man who was so hopeless with a sword.

Sebastian has never seen Sir Toby before and is confused. As Sir Toby struggles to throw Sebastian out, Olivia comes along and sees Sebastian – she too thinks this is Viola. She is furious with Sir Toby and sends him off in disgrace.

Olivia is in love with Sebastian. He very quickly learns to love her too.

Oh what confusion, what a tangle, what a jumble. Olivia loved the boy Caesario who was not a boy but a girl, Viola. Viola loves Orsino but Orsino loves Olivia. Malvolio loves Lady Olivia too. Now Olivia loves Sebastian, who she thinks is Caesario, and Sebastian loves her.

But Malvolio has been locked away in a cell where Sir Toby torments him and where Malvolio begs someone to let him write to Olivia and explain. He no longer

thinks Lady Olivia loves him. So that part on the twisted tale is sorted.

Olivia marries Sebastian, suddenly and in secret. So that part of the tangle is sorted too.

Now we wait to see how Viola – dressed as Caesario – can find happiness with Duke Orsino... and find even more happiness by meeting the brother she thinks is dead.

The girl's tale

The Queen was laughing so much she didn't notice her little maid slip out of the great hall. As I ran up the stairs to the servants' room I explained to John. 'I want to give the bodyguards messages. But no one will believe a girl. If I dress as a boy it may work.'

John passed me a suit of servant's clothes — shirt, jacket, stockings and breeches. I kept my own shoes as his were far too large... and I may need to run.

Then we hurried down to the library, took some paper, pens and ink, and I wrote the messages. I told John what he had to do.

There were two doors into the great hall and two of the Earl of Essex's men stood at each door as silent and wooden as the doorposts. They watched the Queen, not the play.

I watched John whisper in the ear of the one with a brown-bear beard. I knew what he was saying. 'The Queen wants you to give the Earl a special bottle of French wine and two silver cups. One cup for her, one for the Earl. They are in the wine cellar in the palace. Will you fetch them?'

'Why me?' the man growled. 'Why can't

you get them?'

'There's a label on the wine bottle. It says it's a special gift to the Queen's favourite earl.'

'So fetch it.'

'I don't know which bottle it is.'

'Read the label,' the man sighed.

'I can't read,' John said with a shrug. 'But I have the keys to the cellar. Follow me and I'll show you.'

The man followed. I watched as John led the way down cold, dark steps to the wine cellar and unlocked the door. He handed the bearded guard a candle from the wall and let him in through the thick oak door. As soon as the man stepped inside John shut the door and locked it.

'He hurried back to where I was waiting. 'Just like Malvolio,' I said with a grin. 'Locked away in a cellar. One bodyguard gone... three to go.'

Brothers and bruises

The girl's tale

I handed John a note for the guard who sat by himself – the young one with long fair hair. I crept through the torch-shadows to the grey-haired one who sat dozing on a bench with his back against the wall.

I had seen many letters from the Earl of Essex to Her Majesty so I knew his handwriting and I had copied it – just as the maid Maria had copied Olivia's handwriting to write the note Malvolio found.

I also had a piece of rope. I checked the letter one last time. It read...

One of my guards is a traitor. I will send him to the front gate. As soon as you get this message go to the gate, arrest him, tie him up and gag him. I trust you.

Essex

John gave a note to the fair-haired guard. I gave a note to the grey-haired one. Of course it was exactly the same note. Just like the way Maria and Sir Andrew, the makers of mischief, made two people think they had to fight one another.

Both men looked shocked. Both slipped from their seats and headed to the gateway of the palace. When they arrived they cried, 'I arrest you, traitor!'

Both replied, 'No... I arrest YOU.'

Then each began a struggle to tie the other up. It could take all night. John and I went back in to see the end of the play. I left John standing by the suit of armour

with the mace that had filled me with fear. Three guards gone. One to go.

The torches crackled and the play was coming to a happy end... for some of the characters.

The play

At last Countess Olivia meets Duke Orsino. And there, in the Duke's court, is Viola. Olivia thinks it is her new husband, Sebastian, and is hurt when Viola says she is true to Orsino and they start to leave.

'Caesario, my husband, stay,' Olivia begs.

'Your husband?' Duke Orsino says.

'Yes, you are my husband, aren't you?' Olivia asks Viola.

'Are you?' Orsino asks.

'I'm not,' Viola cries.

Olivia sends for the priest who married

her to the man she thought was Caesario. 'Is this the man I married?' she asks.

'It is,' the priest agrees.

Orsino turns on Viola, angry. 'You young liar. Get out of my sight and never come to my palace again.'

Viola is in despair, Olivia is sunk in misery and Orsino is deep in gloom. How will it end? It ends in the strangest way. Sir Andrew enters with Sir Toby Belch, both beaten and bleeding. Limp Sir Andrew sobs to Olivia, 'Your young friend Caesario did this to me. We thought he was a coward but he is a devil.'

Everyone is puzzled. How could Caesario do this when he has been here all the time?

That's when Sebastian rushes in. He hurries to Olivia's side. 'I'm sorry I hurt your Uncle Toby... I was defending myself.'

But no one is listening to what he is saying. They are just amazed to see the twins together at last. **'Same face, same clothes, same voice,'** Orsino gasps. 'But two people. How can this be possible?'

Viola looks at him in wonder. 'My brother? You're not drowned.'

'My sister?' Sebastian laughs. 'You're not drowned.'

And then the tangle all comes clear. Olivia has her Sebastian. Orsino sees Viola as a lovely girl and says he'll marry her. Even Sir Toby says he'll marry the lively serving maid Maria and settle down.

Sir Andrew is bruised and loveless. Olivia forgives Malvolio and has him let out of his prison cell. He is free but the chief servant is in a rage. **'I'll have my revenge on the whole pack of you,'** he cries.

Of course he won't. For this is one story that will end happily for almost everyone.

The girl's tale

The play ended and the audience clapped. I passed the final note to the last of the Earl's guards... a thin man with a face scarred from many battles. His face was sunburned and hard as oak. The message said...

A change of plan. When the play ends stand outside the door in front of the suit of armour.

Essex

I stood in the doorway so I could see into the passage with the suit of armour. The man of oak stood there with his hand on his dagger, ready to fight.

He heard a slight creak from behind him. He turned he looked up. He tried to step away but was too late. The heavy mace in the armour hand came down and cracked him on the skull. He fell in a heap on the stone floor. He would be harmless for many hours. John stepped from behind the armour with a grin on his face.

Inside the hall the Earl of Essex looked worried. Where were his guards when he needed them? I could have told him a maid of the Queen and a wine server had defeated them... with the help of Mr Shakespeare's play.

The plotting Earl rose to his feet to make his speech – the one where he would tell the nobles he was taking over the throne. The audience fell silent. His lips moved but the words were not the ones he meant to speak. 'We... we would like to thank Her Majesty for inviting us to see this wonderful play.'

The audience clapped again – the Queen rose to her feet and hobbled from the room. And as for the Twelfth Night rebellion? No one ever knew how a maid and a serving boy saved the Queen.

The true story

The Earl of Essex was a foolish and boastful man. In February 1601 he gathered a small army of fighting friends and rode through the streets of London. He called for the people of London to support him... the people of London said, 'No thank you!' and Essex looked a bit silly. The Queen's soldiers arrested him.

Essex said, 'Sorry,' to Elizabeth.

Elizabeth said, 'You will be.' His neck went to the block, the axe went on his neck.

In 'Twelfth Night' Olivia was miserable

when she thought her husband had betrayed her. And Elizabeth was just as heartbroken when Essex let her down. She grew weaker and more unhappy. Two years later she died. The last of the Tudor kings and queens.

Did you know?

Twelfth Night was written for the Twelfth Night of Christmas – probably 1601. Queen Elizabeth I would die just two years later. She was growing very old and wouldn't go out to the theatre. Master Shakespeare's players would have taken the play to her palace.

Shakespeare's plays had very little scenery and no lighting - the plays were usually set up in the open air and performed in daylight. Yet this didn't stop him from doing exciting and spectacular scenes.

In *The Tempest*, for example, the play opens with a ship-wreck and in *Twelfth Night* survivors of a storm appear on a rocky beach. The stage helpers would be thumping sheets of metal backstage to make the sounds of a storm while the actors would be rushing around, shouting and panicking as if their ship was going down. The water, the ship and the storm were all in Shakespeare's words and in the imaginations of the spectators.

Shakespeare's stage was almost empty. It was nowhere... so it could quickly become anywhere.

Twelfth Night is a comedy, but a very cruel one. The main joke involves driving a pompous (but pathetic) man insane. Not really funny at all.

What next?

In this tale the Earl of Essex is told, 'You can't come in here,' because he was wearing a sword.

In *Twelfth Night* Viola is told, 'You can't come in here,' because Lady Olivia is in a grumpy mood.

Most of us meet someone, at some time, who says, 'You can't come in here.' What can you do about it?

You can be a bully and try to force your way in, like the Earl of Essex would. Or you could try to 'persuade' the person on the door that they should let you in. Viola says she will camp out at the gates of Olivia's palace till she let her in. She says she will...

Make me a willow cabin at your gate.

She says she'll write poems and sing sad songs till Olivia feels sorry for her and opens the door. Can YOU persuade someone to let you in?

Either:

a) Work with a friend and pretend that one of you is shut out OR

b) Write a letter to your friend telling them why they should let you in.

Now try these...

1. You want to get the bus home from school but the ticket is 25p and you only have 20p. The driver won't let you on unless you 'persuade' him. (Starting point: you may not be safe, walking home alone.)

2. You want to see a movie but the manager of the cinema says you are too young. 'Persuade' her. (Starting point: you look young but are really old enough.)

3. Imagine you are the Earl of Essex. What can you say to the guard who wants to keep you out? Can you 'persuade' him? (Starting point: you are the queen's favourite and she will be angry if you are kept out.)

4. Imagine you are Viola. What words will you use to 'persuade' Olivia to let you in? If she won't see you can you write her a letter?

Terry Deary's Shakespeare Tales

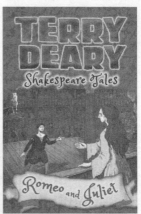

If you liked this book
why not look out for the rest of
Terry Deary's Shakespeare Tales?
Meet Shakespeare and his
theatre company!

World War I Tales

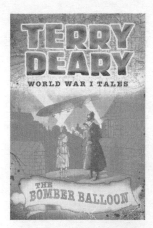

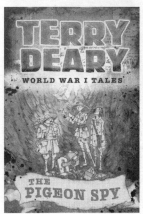

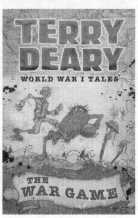

Exciting, funny stories based on real events . . . welcome to World War I!

World War II Tales

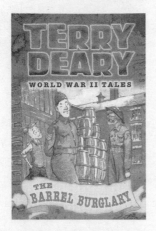

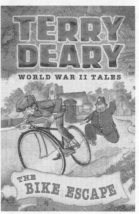

Exciting, funny stories based on real events...
welcome to World War II!